S0-BZP-196

CHARLIE BROWN'S
Two-Minute Stories

Peanuts® characters created and drawn by CHARLES M. SCHULZ

Text by MARGO LUNDELL
Background illustrations by ART and KIM ELLIS

A GOLDEN BOOK • NEW YORK
Western Publishing Company, Inc., Racine, Wisconsin 53404

Copyright © 1988 United Feature Syndicate, Inc. All rights reserved. Printed in the U.S.A. No part of this book may be reproduced or copied in any form without written permission from the publisher. GOLDEN®, GOLDEN & DESIGN®, and A GOLDEN BOOK® are trademarks of Western Publishing Company, Inc. Library of Congress Catalog Card Number: 87-83204 ISBN: 0-307-12185-2/ISBN: 0-307-62185-5 (lib. bdg.)   C D E F G H I J K L M

Schroeder's Helpful Friends

One sunny afternoon Lucy was talking to Charlie Brown.

"I think we owe it to Schroeder," Lucy said. "Being a brilliant pianist isn't easy, Charlie Brown. If Schroeder wants our help to get through the recital, then we should give it to him."

Charlie Brown agreed to help, but he wondered if Lucy's feelings about Schroeder had anything to do with her plan. Everybody knew that Lucy was crazy about him.

"I have to go now," Lucy said as she rushed off. "I have to think of ways we can help Schroeder."

The next day Lucy went to Schroeder's house and began cleaning his practice room. "All this dust might make you cough," she told him.

"You shouldn't bother, Lucy," said Schroeder. He wished he could just get on with his practicing.

"But I *love* dusting pianos," Lucy said sweetly. "It makes my fingers tingle."

Then she took out an air freshener and sprayed the room. Schroeder sighed. He couldn't wait for Lucy to leave him alone!

Schroeder's troubles continued. Each afternoon Lucy sent someone over to help him while he practiced.

Charlie Brown tried to keep Schroeder company, but he couldn't resist trying out his new kite at the same time.

One afternoon Schroeder found himself staring into the eyes of Ludwig van Beagle, who offered him tips on how to play the piano.

Even Woodstock came to tweet along with the music one afternoon, but he made it rather difficult to practice.

Schroeder grew more and more nervous. His friends were interrupting him so often that he had no time to practice. Finally he began having nightmares. He dreamed that Lucy took his piano to the Laundromat. When she brought it back, the piano had shrunk.

The next day Schroeder called everybody over to his house and asked them to stop helping him. "The truth is, I never asked for any help at all," he said.

Charlie Brown looked at Lucy. "You said he wanted our help." Lucy walked out of the room in a huff.

"Come on, everybody," Charlie Brown said to the others. "Let's leave Schroeder alone so he can practice!"

The next day was the recital. Schroeder played very well. Even Lucy admitted he had done a fine job.

"That *was* the best I've ever played," said Schroeder. "Maybe it was better that I didn't spend so much time practicing and tiring myself out. I guess I should thank you, Lucy," he said. "I couldn't have done it without your help."

For the first time ever, Lucy was speechless.

Puppy Love

One morning Charlie Brown was complaining to Linus. "There just isn't enough time to do everything," he said. "For instance, my mother bought a shoe box full of old baseball cards for me at a rummage sale, and I haven't had time to sort them."

"Hold it, Charlie Brown," said Linus, staring across the street. "Isn't that Marcie hiding behind the mailbox?"

"AARGH!" said Charlie Brown. "She's after me again!"

It was true. Marcie was following Charlie Brown. At school she was there each day at lunchtime, offering him little boxes of raisins. After school he could feel a shadow following him home.

One evening when he went out the back door of his house to feed Snoopy, Charlie Brown thought he saw Marcie peering at him from behind the bushes.

On Saturday, as Charlie Brown was about to walk out to the baseball mound, Marcie appeared out of nowhere. "Good luck, Charlie Brown," she said. Then she kissed him on the cheek!

Charlie Brown asked Linus for advice. He couldn't stand to have
Marcie following him anymore. "How can I get her to stop?" he said.

"I guess she has a crush on you," said Linus. "In that case, you
shouldn't run away. Instead, you should invite Marcie to spend the whole
day with you. That will scare her off."

"Are you sure?" asked Charlie Brown. "If she thinks I have a crush on
her, my life is over!"

"Trust me," said Linus.

Charlie Brown went to Marcie's house and invited her to spend the day sorting baseball cards with him. "We'll need the whole day," he said. "It will probably take about ten hours."

Then Charlie Brown added, "We can spend tomorrow looking at my stamp collection, and the day after that..." he continued.

Marcie looked pale. "I'm busy tomorrow," she said, backing into her house. "I have to go now. I can hear my mother calling." Marcie shut the door in Charlie Brown's face.

That night Charlie Brown called Linus to thank him for the good advice.

"That's OK," said Linus. "Here's how you can pay me back. I have this shoe box full of baseball cards that needs sorting. I'll bring it over tomorrow so you can start."

"Good grief!" said Charlie Brown. "Two boxes of baseball cards! Now I'm sorry that Marcie *isn't* coming over to help me tomorrow."

What's Wrong, Snoopy?

"I think something's bothering Snoopy," Charlie Brown said to Lucy. "He hasn't been eating very much lately."

Lucy shook her head. "Knowing you, Charlie Brown, you're probably giving him cat food by mistake, or maybe parakeet treats."

"I am not!" said Charlie Brown. "It's dog food, the same stuff I always feed him. He's just eating less of it."

Charlie Brown decided to try to pep up Snoopy's appetite. In the next few days he tried everything he could think of to interest his dog in food. He pretended to be Snoopy's personal waiter, offering a special menu that listed Dogue Food Fondue, Boeuf à la Charles, and other wonderful choices.

Nothing worked. Finally Charlie Brown sprinkled chocolate-chip cookies over Snoopy's food. When that didn't make any difference either, Charlie Brown decided Snoopy must be sick. He planned to take him to the vet the very next day.

The next morning Charlie Brown had to hunt all over town to find his dog. At last he spotted him on the playing field behind the school. Snoopy and the Beagle Scouts were in the middle of a Beagle Master's Fitness Contest. They had trained hard for the event, and they won the competition.

After the medals had been awarded, Charlie Brown decided not to take Snoopy to the vet. He figured that Snoopy's appetite would probably return to normal now that he was no longer in training.

Charlie Brown was right. That night Snoopy ate with his usual appetite. For the first time in days Snoopy wasn't counting calories and doing push-ups out behind the doghouse. Instead, Snoopy chose his favorite dish—pizza and chocolate-chip cookies, of course!

What Did You Say?

One winter Charlie Brown and his friends caught colds and had to stay home from school. All around town kids were sneezing and sniffling. Since they couldn't get together, the school pals talked on the phone.

Charlie Brown and Linus were on the phone one day when Charlie Brown happened to mention Harold Angel, one of their friends. Harold had a crush on Charlie Brown's sister, Sally, and Charlie Brown was sick of seeing Harold hanging around the house.

"I'm fed up," said Charlie Brown. "I'm fed up with ol' Hal."

Linus was very sad when he got off the phone. Not only was he sick and sneezing, but he had just lost his best friend.

"He's fed up with me," Linus said sadly. "Charlie Brown said he's fed up with his ol' pal."

Linus didn't realize he had misunderstood his friend. Because of his cold, Linus's ears were clogged and he wasn't hearing very well.

Then the phone rang. It was Marcie, calling about makeup assignments for school. Marcie was home with a cold, too. Linus sadly told her about his conversation with Charlie Brown.

After she hung up, Marcie felt wonderful in spite of her cold. "What great news!" she said to herself. "Charlie Brown is fed up with his ol' gal. I don't know who his old girlfriend was, but I'm glad he's fed up with her!"

Marcie blew her nose. Then she called Peppermint Patty to tell her the great news, but Peppermint Patty wasn't impressed. She had a cold like everyone else, and she wasn't hearing clearly.

"Chuck's little sister always bugs him," Peppermint Patty said to herself after she hung up with Marcie. "What's the big deal if he's fed up with ol' Sal?"

Just then Sally happened to call Peppermint Patty.

"I hear your brother is fed up with you," said Peppermint Patty sympathetically. "I guess you were fighting with him."

Sally was furious when she hung up the phone. She was the only one who didn't have a cold, and she had heard Peppermint Patty *very* clearly.

"Charlie Brown, you blockhead!" she shouted at her brother. "How dare you tell everybody that you're fed up with me! That's the most embarrassing thing that's ever happened to me!"

Charlie Brown had no idea what his sister was talking about. As she shouted at him, he glanced out the window and saw Harold Angel walking up to the front door. Charlie Brown shook his head. Sally was yelling, and now Harold was back.

"Good grief!" he thought. "This just isn't my day!"

Whose Dog Is That?

One day Charlie Brown and Snoopy watched as a moving van drove past and parked halfway down the block. Then the movers got out and began unloading the truck.

"I guess we're going to have new neighbors," said Charlie Brown. "I hope they have kids."

Snoopy rolled his eyes. "I hope they *don't* have cats!" he thought.

In the days that followed, Snoopy went about his business as usual. He played a round of golf with his trusty caddie.

The Flying Ace flew a daring mission one morning and then walked to his favorite bistro to have lunch.

During his outings up and down the block Snoopy was being watched by the new neighbors. They had never seen a dog like Snoopy before. Each day they asked each other in amazement, "Whose dog is that, anyway?"

Then one night the new neighbors went over to Charlie Brown's house for a backyard barbecue. Charlie Brown's parents were trying to make the new neighbors feel welcome.

The new neighbors saw Snoopy and gasped. That was the very dog that had paraded past their house every day! Now he seemed to be a normal dog, standing on all four feet and eating dog food from a bowl.

The new neighbors looked at each other. "Maybe we need our eyes checked," they thought. "We must have been seeing things."

As they turned away, Snoopy climbed up on his doghouse. "I always do my best work on a full stomach," thought the world's greatest author as he sat down in front of his typewriter.

Poor Peppermint Patty

The last day of school was over. Summer vacation had just begun.
Instead of kicking up her heels, Peppermint Patty was down in the dumps.

"I know I failed the test today," she told Charlie Brown. "I bet I didn't
even get a D minus. I'll have to stay back next year. It's hopeless."

"Cheer up, Peppermint Patty," said Charlie Brown. "At least we don't
have any homework tonight!"

Nevertheless, Peppermint Patty was very sad. She went straight home and turned on the television.

"Dad won't be home for a while," she said to herself. "I'll just sit here and feel awful until he gets home."

The phone rang, but Peppermint Patty didn't answer it. "It's probably my teacher," she thought. "She's calling to tell me I really did fail."

The phone rang again. "That's probably Chuck," Peppermint Patty said. "He's calling to tell me he doesn't want to be friends with anybody as dumb as me."

Then the doorbell rang. Peppermint Patty didn't answer it. "It's probably my teacher again," she thought. "She wants me to know I'm being thrown out of school."

Then Peppermint Patty heard a scratching sound at the front door. She went to look out the window and saw Woodstock. He was holding an envelope.

Peppermint Patty gave in. She opened the door to see what Woodstock had brought her.

Peppermint Patty couldn't believe her eyes. On the front porch was a big bunch of flowers from Charlie Brown. Woodstock handed her the card. It said:

Dear Peppermint Patty,
    I hope these flowers will cheer you up. Don't worry—
I just know that you passed the test.

Your friend,
Charlie Brown

Then Peppermint Patty found another note on the steps. It was from her teacher, saying that she hadn't failed the test after all. Peppermint Patty almost fainted with relief.

"Thanks, Woodstock," she said to her little yellow friend. "If it hadn't been for you, I'd be watching television for the rest of my life."

Then she ran down the block to find all her friends and begin a fun summer vacation.

Smile and Say Tweet

It was a bright, sunny day in early spring.

"Gramma says the trailing arbutus is probably blooming," said Sally.

"What's that?" asked Charlie Brown.

"The trailing arbutus is a rare plant that grows deep in the woods and flowers early in the spring," said Sally. "Gramma says hardly anybody can find it."

Snoopy's ears perked up. Find the trailing arbutus? It sounded like an excellent challenge for the Beagle Master. Call the scouts! Prepare for a hike!

Early the next morning the troop headed into the woods. After the Beagle Master came the scouts—Woodstock, Bill, Conrad, and Olivier.

The hikers had brought their new cameras with them. They were so excited snapping pictures, they hardly noticed they were in the woods.

Snoopy was exasperated with the scouts. "We're on a mission, Beagle Scouts!" he said. "Now, let's get going!"

For hours Snoopy kept a beagle eye out for the rare little plant described in the guide book. At last he was convinced he had found it, but the scouts paid no attention at all. They were still twittering and giggling and posing for each other. Snoopy decided to dig up the plant and head for home.

Suddenly he stopped. "I can't dig up that plant!" Snoopy thought. "I have to leave the woods the way I find them. Besides, this is a rare species."

Snoopy shook his head. What bad luck! Now he wouldn't have anything to show Charlie Brown's grandmother.

Then Snoopy had a brilliant idea. "The cameras!" he thought.
The Beagle Master lined up the silly scouts and told them to take
pictures of the little flowering plant.

Later, when the rolls of film were developed, Snoopy gathered together
87 pictures of trailing arbutus. He gave 86 of them to Charlie Brown's
grandmother. Woodstock wanted the last picture for his forest photo album.
He called the collection "Taking Stock of the Woods—Photos by
Woodstock!"

Cheer Up, Charlie Brown

Snoopy couldn't help but notice. "The round-headed kid is having a tough summer," he said to himself.

It was a fact. Charlie Brown was miserable. He couldn't seem to get ahead that summer.

The few tennis balls he managed to hit landed miles away.

The baseballs he actually whacked were so rare, they became collector's items.

The pond he swam in was only knee-deep.

The last straw for Charlie Brown was losing to Snoopy at checkers. Poor Charlie Brown couldn't even win playing against his own dog.

Then Snoopy decided to take action. The next night he waited for Charlie Brown to bring out his dinner as usual.

Charlie Brown was about to put Snoopy's food down when he saw the blue ribbon pinned to the doghouse. Then he read what it said and smiled.

FOR CHARLIE BROWN
NUMBER ONE
BEST BEAGLE FEEDER

1

"And you're the best beagle in the world," Charlie Brown said as he gave Snoopy a hug.